Presented by:

_____

To:

_____

Date:

_____

Occasion:

_____

We Have Seen
a Great Light

"99 Words to Live By"

A series of fine gift books that presents inspirational words by renowned authors and captivating thinkers. Thought-provoking proverbs from many peoples and traditions complete each volume's collection.

"99 Words to Live By" explores topics that have moved and will continue to move people's hearts. Perfect for daily reflection as well as moments of relaxation.

We Have Seen
a Great Light

99 Sayings
on Christmas

edited by
Alfred Hartl

New City Press
Hyde Park, New York

Published in the United States by New City Press
202 Cardinal Rd., Hyde Park, NY 12538
©2007 New City Press (English translation)

Translated by the NCP editorial staff
from the original German edition
Ein Stern ist mir ins Herz gefallen
©1998 Verlag Neue Stadt, Munich.

Cover design by Leandro De Leon

Library of Congress Cataloging-in-Publication Data:

Stern ist mir ins Herz gefallen. English
    We have seen a great light : 99 sayings on Christmas /
Alfred Hartl, editor.
        p. cm. -- (99 words to live by)
    ISBN 978-1-56548-270-8 (hardcover : alk. paper) --
ISBN 978-1-56548-271-5 (pbk. : alk. paper) 1. Christmas.
I. Hartl, Alfred. II. Title.
BV45.S7813 2007
263'.915--dc22   2007011011

Printed in United States of America

Christmas: How many feelings, how many expectations and longings are connected to this feast. We celebrate it year after year, all over the world, and not only among Christians. It is a unique phenomenon, a sign that the star of Bethlehem can reach all people, that God became man for everyone.

The birth that we celebrate at Christmas is more than a historic memory. It is the center, the abiding message of this feastday: The creator of space and time delimits himself to a small "here" and "now." God does not only help us from his distant heavens. In Jesus he becomes one of us, learns to speak and understand our language, to think our thoughts, to experience our joy and our pain. God becoming man is not one of many events. What happened that night in Bethlehem has no comparison in the history of humanity. Throughout twenty centuries men and women have tried to discover its meaning. Some of them appear in this book, like rays of that Star that never ceases to shine.

Alfred Hartl

What is Christmas?

It is the most
intriguing story
ever told.

Charles Péguy

The most important day
in human history
was not when the first man
set foot on the moon
but when God's Son
came on earth.

James B. Irwin

In those days Caesar Augustus published a decree ordering a census of the whole world. This first census took place while Quirinius was governor of Syria. Everyone went to register, each to his own town. And so Joseph went from the town of Nazareth in Galilee to Judea, to David's town of Bethlehem — because he was of the house and lineage of David — to register with Mary, his espoused wife, who was with child. While they were there the days of her confinement were completed. She gave birth to her first-born son and wrapped him in swaddling clothes and laid him in a manger, because there was no room for them in the place where travelers lodged.

Luke

3

The people
who live in darkness
have seen a great light,
and a light shines over those
who live in the land of
darkness.

From the book of Isaiah

Our Redeemer
was born today,
we must celebrate
with festive joy.
We cannot be sad today
because it is the birthday
of life.

Leo the Great

God's Word
became human
to accustom human beings
to receiving God.
God has begun
to live with the human race.

Irenaeus

With the coming
of God's Word,
motherly love
has embraced us all.

Hildegard of Bingen

Every year, as we start to think of Christmas, the world is bathed in a warm current of love. It is a celebration of joy and love. This is the star toward which all of us are moving.

Edith Stein

What this unique Christian feast aims to do is to give us a deep conviction and a firm faith in one great truth: When God came down from heaven to earth for us he did so because he loves us. When someone loves us, life becomes easier for us and we can understand everything more clearly.

Chiara Lubich

In the most basic sense, Christmas never changes. Over the centuries, despite the many traditions we have added to this day, the central fact remains: God almighty, the eternal One, creator of heaven and earth, becomes human.

Joseph Cardinal Bernardin

Long before we had any hope in ourselves, God had great hope and confidence in us.... God has put his Son into our hands. And that is the ultimate sign of his confidence, trust, and hope.

Joseph Cardinal Bernardin

The warmth of Christmas leads us to feel more like a family, more truly one, more like brothers and sisters, who share everything: joys and suffering.

Chiara Lubich

God's Christmas
is filled with messengers:
one is on his way to you too.

Albrecht Goes

Christmas gives us the key that opens some of the deep mysteries of our existence ...

Why pain? Why humiliation? Why do the "least" of this world have to suffer so much? This is what humanity asked God, but God was silent....

Now, finally, in the Christmas event, God speaks. Now humanity is silent and asks no more qeustions. We hear the story of God's mercy. God is small as he comes into our world; he enters history; he becomes a child in the manger.

Leonardo Boff

14

In God
human pain;
in human beings
God's joy!
What was foreign
to both
is now
their own.

John of the Cross

Christmas means: He has come. He has illuminated the night. He has made the night of our darkness, the night of our lack of understanding, the cruel night of our fears and our hopelessness into Christmas, the holy night.

In the Word made flesh, God has sent his last Word, his most profound Word, his most beautiful Word into the world. And that Word means: I love you, world and humanity. Light the candles! They have more right to be here than darkness.

Karl Rahner

The night is bright.
God has prepared a feast
that did not exist in heaven:
he became man.

Karl Rahner

Of every other child that is born into the world, friends can say that it resembles his mother. Christmas was the first instance in time that anyone could say that the mother resembled the child. This is the beautiful paradox of the child who made his mother; the mother, too, was only a child. It was also the first time in the history of this world that anyone could ever think of heaven as being anywhere else than "somewhere up there"; when the child was in her arms, Mary now looked down to heaven.

Fulton J. Sheen

Since this holy night
God has been
in this world
and the world
has been in God.

Odo Casel

A light has come from Bethlehem that has continued to enlighten the hearts of men and women. The angels' message again and again gives us new hope. Centuries have passed since then and so much has happened to make us lose heart — wars and disasters and disappointments of every kind. But that good news, the grace of that child and the happiness of that mother have continued to help people and nations to free themselves from the night in which they again and again have found themselves straying.

Igino Giordani

One day
there will be no more night
because the night
has turned into Christmas.

Karl Rahner

When God became human, humanity became "God's space" and men and women became related to God and Christ's brothers and sisters. If God became one of us in Jesus, that is surely something that we can never value highly enough. We can place all our human hopes on him. If Jesus is at the same time both God and our brother, then I should never know fear again.

Carlo Carretto

Christmas opens my heart to the whole of humanity. Its warmth goes beyond the Christian world and seems to invade every land, a sign that this baby came for everyone.

Chiara Lubich

In many hearts
darkened by life's pain
shines the light
of Christmas joy,
and teaches them
to look up
and believe again
in the light.

M. Hunnius

The peak of night
is the beginning of day.
The peak of pain
is the beginning of light.

Traditional Christmas Hymn

You are with us, Emmanuel. You are with us as a human being, as a new-born child, weak and vulnerable, wrapped in swaddling cloths and lying in a crib "because there was no place for them at the inn." Could you ever have done any more than you did to be our Emmanuel, God with us?

John Paul II

You wanted to be God,
although you were human
and so you were lost.
He wanted to be human,
although he was God,
so that he could look
for what was lost.
Your human pride
struck you down
with such force
that only the humility of God
could raise you up again.

Augustine of Hippo

I myself am very glad that the divine child was born in a stable, because my soul is very much like a stable, filled with strange unsatisfied longings, with guilt and animal-like impulses, tormented by anxiety, inadequacy and pain. If the holy One could be born in such a place, he can be born in me also. I am not excluded.

Morton Kelsey

To discover
in the stable of Bethlehem
that God is near:
this may restore meaning
to the Christmas feast.

Helmut Thielicke

God becomes a baby to tell us that he is not far away.

The angels are still singing: peace on earth to all people. Let us ask your defenseless omnipotence to bend down and to snuff out the arrogance of violence, to remove hatred from all hearts, replacing it with love, so that soon no nation in the world may remember what war is.

Chiara Lubich

God's Son
became human
so that human beings
might have
their home in God.

Hildegard of Bingen

A homecoming:
that is the gift
which the child of Bethlehem
wants to bestow
on all those
who mourn and weep,
who keep watch
as they walk the earth.

Friedrich von Bodelschwingh

Advent and Christmas
are like a keyhole
through which a ray
of light from home shines
and brightens our path.

Friedrich von Bodelschwingh

Light does not mean that there is no more night. But it does mean that the night is bright and can be overcome.

Heinrich Fries

34

God became human. We did not become God. The human dispensation continues and it must continue. But it is consecrated. And we have become more. We have also been strengthened. Let us trust our life, then, because this night has brought us light. Let us trust life, because we do not live it alone. God lives it with us.

Alfred Delp, S.J.

The star of Bethlehem
is a star
in the darkness of night
even today.

Edith Stein

The Lord
did not come into the world
for us to become smarter
but more merciful.
Therefore only the power
of the heart
can possibly save us again.

Heinrich Waggerl

Our life begins
with the child
in the manger.

Johannes Hanselmann

In the crib, Jesus radiates what the world so much needs today — gentleness, tenderness, light and hope.

Gentleness — as the answer to all violence.

Tenderness — as the answer to the lack of goodness, benevolence and love of our brothers and sisters.

Light — as the answer to the shadows that darken the present time.

Hope — as the answer to those who feel abandoned or who find no meaning in their lives.

Little Sister Magdeleine of Jesus

For long before I came to be, you came with saving grace to choose me from eternity before I knew your face. Even before your molding hand had fashioned me, your love had planned how you would shape my future.

Paul Gerhardt

Before the manger
we are united
with everyone scattered
throughout the world,
and even beyond the world.
This is a mystery
that consoles us.

Edith Stein

Leave to the nativity scenes their naïvety so that all little — and grown-up — children can warm their hearts through them.

Little Sister Magdeleine of Jesus

He became a child so that you could become a full mature human being. He was wrapped in swaddling cloths so that you could be unravelled from the meshes of death. He came on earth so that you could live beneath the stars. There was no place for him in the inn so that there could be many dwelling places for you in heaven. He was rich, but he became poor for us. His poverty is our riches and his weakness is our strength. He is poor for us, but in himself he is rich. You can see him lying there in swaddling cloths, but what you cannot see is that he is God's Son.

Ambrose

The stable of Jesus' birth reminds us that he is a very different kind of king — one born in poverty, one who comes to serve and not to be served. It is this kind of Messiah we are called to follow — to serve others, be light for others. And we take comfort and courage in the belief that Jesus is "Emmanuel" — "God with us" — to guide our feet into the path of peace.

James McGinnis

Jesus was a surprise,
the likes of whom
no one expected.

Joseph Ratzinger
(Pope Benedict XVI)

No one can tell that the child in the manger is Jesus, the son of God. God is hidden in the child. He appears incognito. This is part of the mystery of Christmas: majesty acquires lowliness; power, weakness; eternity, mortality. God comes silently. He does not advertise his power. The events in the stable and the manger secretely foreshadow the cross of Golgotha.

Karl Lehmann

He doesn't ask questions
He doesn't blame you
He knows you
He smiles at you
He loves you
This is the mystery
of Christmas.

Wolfgang Poeplau

Child, dear child,
help me to discover
in both the most earnest
and the most severe people
the child asleep in their hearts.

Helder Camara

Children live completely
out of and in trust.
Children know no mistrust.
To heal the hearts
of mistrusting
men and women
God gives us a child.

Carlo Maria Martini

The divine child
fulfills the promise.
It is only where he is awaited
that he is received.
Otherwise no child
is born for us tonight.
But where he is accepted
he exceeds every expectation.

Jean-Marie Lustiger

To become human means to become like a child. Ever since Adam and Eve there has been no exception to this. The way to humanity leads through the child. It is the very way God has chosen. God's Son has become man by becoming a child....

Only who becomes like a child enters the kingdom of God, by being simple and pure, by feeling for others and being joyful, by receiving gifts and giving gifts.

The child: healing from resignation and calculation.

Klaus Hemmerle

God comes into our midst as a child. He gives us an example of the complete trust typical of children. He trusts us so much that he gives us what is most precious to him, his defenseless Son.

Carlo Maria Martini

When you became small,
O God, you made
human beings great.

Catherine of Siena

God made great
what was small
and approachable
and comprehensible
what was great.

Joseph Ratzinger
(Pope Benedict XVI)

God becomes man. He suffers with us. He does not answer the "why" of suffering but becomes himself a man of suffering.

And thus we are not alone in our loneliness. He is with us. We are no longer lonely but in solidarity with one another. Our intellect is silent and our heart begins to speak. It tells the story of a God who became a child; who does not ask questions but acts; who does not answer with words but with his life.

Leonardo Boff

God's becoming human
is not an idyll;
it is a scandal!

Klaus Hemmerle

God
was incomprehensible,
inapproachable, invisible,
and hard to imagine.
He became man,
came close to us
in a manger
so that we could see
and understand him.

Bernard of Clairvaux

If your Word
had not become flesh
and had not dwelt
among us,
we would have had
to believe
that there was
no connection
between God
and humanity
and we would
have been in despair.

Augustine of Hippo

God sent the world
no technical assistance
no angel Gabriel
accompanied with experts
no food or used clothing ...

Rather he came himself
born in a stable
hungry in the desert
naked on the cross.
He shared with us
and became our bread,
he suffered with us
and became our peace.

From Hong Kong

This is the message
of Christmas:
God comes to meet us,
regardless of where we are.

Helmut Thielicke

In order to finally make himself understood, God came among us on Christmas Day through Jesus Christ, poor and low. Had Jesus not lived among us, God would still be unreachable.

Roger Schutz

The creator of man
became man
so that he the Bread
could be hungry;
the Fountain
could be thirsty;
Power
could become weak;
Salvation
could be wounded;
Life
could die.

Augustine of Hippo

Today
we can understand
the depth of God's
concern for us.
Today we can experience
what he thinks of us.

Bernard of Clairvaux

Gold, friend, power and honor — nothing can make us so happy as the joyful news that Christ became man. The human heart can scarcely conceive it and we can certainly not talk enough about it. To do such a thing and let us hear about it, God must love us with all his heart. He must love me because he comes so close to me, because he became human with me. He became what I am.

Martin Luther

"The kindness and generous love of God our savior appeared" (Tit 3:4) — that is one of the Christmas proclamations. So it is possible for the stable of our life, the rubble and debris and frighteningly frigid storms of fate to become the time and place for a new holy night, a new birth of the God who searches out and saves us....

Night shall not frighten us nor calamity fatigue us. We will ever watch, wait and call out until the star begins to shine.

Alfred Delp, S.J.

The one
whom no one has ever seen
has shown himself
as he is:
Remaining God
he took on humanity.

Leonardo Boff

We cannot imagine God
in terms that are
human enough.

Romano Guardini

God becoming man
is the great message
of his love.
In it
we humans see
God's face.

Hildegard of Bingen

Jesus came into this world, but he did not tell anyone, even those who were closest to him, who he was. If he had entered the world in his home in Nazareth, his coming might have been celebrated with great rejoicing by all his relatives and by the neighbors and all those who lived in the town. But he was born on a journey and in the midst of a great number of unknown people. So he really does belong to everyone — and he came very reticently, making no noise.... God does not want to thrust his Son upon us. He wants us to come to him. We have to look for him. We have to discover him. Yes, Jesus is infinitely reticent. He waits.

René Voillaume

He is simply there — that is all that he does or that he can do. But, by being there, powerless yet radiant, it is God himself who is there. God is there for us. What, then, does this being God in the child of Bethlehem say to us? It says to me and to you and to every human being: it is good that you are there.

Klaus Hemmerle

I have come
like the word from the heart,
the ray from the sun,
warmth from the fire,
fragrance from the flower
the brook from its
eternal fountain.

Ephraim the Syrian

In his Son God took a heart, a human heart, embued with the love that he himself is and that reaches out to all human challenges and life situations. Anything, anything at all, touches his heart. Whatever happens to us, it is something that touches God's heart.

Klaus Hemmerle

Jesus has come not because we are so good but because he is good. The one who can believe this experiences something of Christmas. If Jesus were born only in Bethlehem but not in our hearts, then we would not know how much we are loved.

Wilfried Hagemann

The Word became flesh. The Word became heart. God accepted a heart. God's heart beats in the countless millions of human hearts. Since then we are able to know what dwells in the heart of humanity, because God who knows everything wanted to be close to everything. Not only did he want to know what is in the heart of humanity — he also wanted to experience it....

It is not just a longing — it is reality. Every heart is a heart that is loved. For every human heart is worth God's own heart and God has offered himself up for every human being.

Klaus Hemmerle

The birthday of the Lord
is the birthday of peace.

Leo the Great

With Christmas the light of peace breaks through into our world and brings the light of joy into our eyes. To fully understand humanity and not to despise it has become possible through God who became man.

Dietrich Bonhoeffer

God does not reserve peace for heaven alone: he wants peace on earth. And he wants us to be the builders of this peace: a peace that will not come from ever more refined weapons, stockpiled all over the world at the expense of the poor. May peace come through us, a peace that is not a result of threats but rather of justice, reconciliation and bold love.

George Moser

Jesus did not come exclusively for people with white skin, nor did he come only for black people. He did not come simply for Europeans or just for people in other parts of the world. Christ became human for the whole of humankind. That means he also came for each one of us. It also means a feast for all of us, joy for all of us and freedom and peace for all of us.

Chiara Lubich

The Lord has sent me to bring good news to the poor. Christmas is the feast of the poor — a very poor feast, the birth of a child who was rejected by everyone. And the first to come to the crib were simple people — shepherds, poor people. They were the first to hear the good news and to be told: "Today the Savior is born for you."

Jean Vanier

The star was right
to stop over the house
of "little" people:
From there
comes a great future.

Klaus Hemmerle

When the King of Kings was born, he chose his parents from among the little people of this world. And the simple people of the district were the first he invited to his cradle — those who slept under the stars of heaven and could hear the angel's voice. It was only then that he received the great ones of the world.... He called them, but they were so far off that the journey took them a long time. Those mighty kings announced their arrival with expensive presents. But first they kneeled down — humility was their real gift. They kneeled down after the shepherds. That is how Christmas was and that is how it will be until the end of the world.

Gilbert Cesbron

Christmas!
On that night
was born in a manger
the poor man
whose love was to shake
the world.
Christmas!
Since that time
no one has the right
to be happy in isolation.

Raoul Follereau

Anyone who has
really understood
that God became human
can never speak and act
in an inhuman way.

Karl Barth

Christmas is an offer to us:
Don't remain alone.
Trust the light
that has started to shine
at Bethlehem also for you.
And follow the call
of your heart
that is happiest
when it can give of itself.

Joachim Wanke

Because God
has become human,
all ways leading to God
go through humans.

Arnold Janssen

When the Word of God became human he certainly adapted himself to life in the world and was baby and child, man and worker. But also he brought the way of life of his heavenly homeland, and he wanted people and objects to be recomposed in a new order, according to the law of heaven: Love.

Chiara Lubich

Christmas is the last word pronounced over us. It tells us that we are loved, that we are free and that we are able to follow the way to God, that we are new-born and can begin again our life and our work of building up society. This word of hope lies behind all the greetings that we send to each other at Christmas. It is the true meaning of all the presents that we send to each other. The child who comes to us is the sign given to us that God has opened the door that leads to this way.

Carlo Maria Martini

Selfgiving
is the new way of being
that is in tune
with Christmas.
Selfgiving is the particular
poverty and wealth
of God, of man,
and of all created beings.
Not a byproduct
but a silent revelation
of the mystery we call love.

Klaus Hemmerle

The gift that God
bestows on us
by making us his children
so that we can call
God "Father"
is the greatest gift of all.

Leo the Great

This is where we find the deeper meaning of the long-established tradition of giving special presents at Christmas, the practice of wanting to give much more than we are able to give or can afford to give. When we go beyond our resources and ability in this way, we become aware that there is something that transcends our ordinary everyday tasks and duties, something that gives us an insight into the nature of the kingdom of God, in which all of us are rich, generous in giving and indeed almost as almighty as God himself.

Hugo Rahner

The true meaning of Christmas is not to be found exclusively in the love of hearth and home, the happiness of children or the family gathering. It can also be celebrated by those who are lonely, who are separated from their family or who simply have no family. Christmas is not just the feast of those who have something to give — it is also the feast of those who have nothing to give or no one to give to. It is not only a family feast — it is also the feast of those who are alone.

Romano Guardini

Christmas means: to live with hope, to reach out to one another in reconciliation, to welcome foreigners, to help one another, to do what is good, and to dry the tears. When one gives love to another, when the plight of the unfortunate is alleviated, when hearts are happy and content, then God descends from heaven and brings the light: then it is Christmas.

Christmas carol from Haiti

Imitate God:
Become human!

Franz Kamphaus

Don't forget:
Miracles are possible!
God
has become man.
People
can be human.
Day after day.

Wolfgang Poeplau

Who is the one who celbrates Christmas properly? It is the one who lays down before the manger all violence, honor, reputation, vanity, pride, egocentricity; the one who is on the side of the lowly and lets God alone be the one on high.

Dietrich Bonhoeffer

Christmas is our feastday. Celebrate the birth by which you were redeemed. Honor the small town of Bethlehem, which has brought you back to paradise. Start out to follow the star and bear gifts along with the Magi.... Praise him with the shepherds and sing songs of joy with the angels....

Let us celebrate this feast together in heaven and on earth. I am convinced that in heaven too there is celebration, because all who dwell there love the God-Man.

Gregory Nazianzen

The three Magi only had a rumor to go by, but it moved them to take on a long journey. The scribes had more knowledge, but it did not move them in any way.

Where, then, was more of the truth to be found? With the three Kings, who followed a rumor, or with the scribes, who took all their knowledge and sat still in silence?

Sören Kierkegaard

Since Bethlehem,
our earth has been
changed for ever.
Since then,
it has borne God's glory.
Since then,
no power has ever been able
to tear this earth
out of God's hands.

Alfred Bengsch

Every day
can be Christmas.

Chiara Lubich

Also available in the same series:

On Our Pilgrimage to Eternity
99 Sayings by John Paul II
hardcover: 1-56548-198-4
softcover: 1-56548-230-1

Words of Hope and Healing
99 Sayings by Henri Nouwen
1-56548-227-1, 112 pp., hardcover

Like a Drop in the Ocean
99 Sayings by Mother Teresa
hardcover: 1-56548-238-7
softcover: 1-56548-242-5

The Path of Merciful Love
99 Sayings by Thérèse of Lisieux
hardcover: 1-56548-245-X
softcover: 1-56548-246-8

Overlook Much, Correct a Little
99 Sayings by John XXIII
hardcover: 978-1-56548-261-6
paperback: 978-1-56548-255-5

Coming Together in Joy
99 Sayings by Benedict XVI
978-1-56548-273-9, 112 pp., hardcover

* * *

The Golden Thread of Life
99 Sayings on Love
1-56548-182-8, 112 pp., hardcover

Blessed Are the Peacemakers
99 Sayings on Peace
1-56548-183-6, 112 pp., hardcover

Sunshine On Our Way
99 Sayings on Friendship
ISBN 1-56548-195-X, 112 pp., hardcover

Organizations and Corporations

This title is available at special quantity discounts for bulk purchases for sales promotions, premiums, or fundraising.

For information call or write:
New City Press, Marketing Dept.
202 Cardinal Rd.
Hyde Park, NY 12538.
Tel: 1-800-462-5980;
1-845-229-0335
Fax: 1-845-229-0351
info@newcitypress.com

NEW CITY PRESS
www.newcitypress.com
1-800-462-5980

**Thank you for choosing this book.
If you would like to receive regular information
about New City Press titles, please fill in this card.**

Title purchased: _____

Please check the subjects that are of particular interest to you:

- ○ **FATHERS OF THE CHURCH**
- ○ **CLASSICS IN SPIRITUALITY**
- ○ **CONTEMPORARY SPIRITUALITY**
- ○ **THEOLOGY**
- ○ **SCRIPTURE AND COMMENTARIES**
- ○ **FAMILY LIFE**
- ○ **BIOGRAPHY / HISTORY**
- ○ **INSPIRATION / GIFT**

Other subjects of interest: _____

(please print)

Name: _____

Address: _____

_____

Telephone: _____

NEW CITY PRESS
202 CARDINAL RD.
HYDE PARK, NY 12538

Place
Stamp
Here